My Weird School Daze #1

Mrs. Dole Is Out of Control!

Dan Gutman

Pictures by

Jim Paillot

HarperTrophy®

An Imprint of HarperCollinsPublishers

To Emma

Mrs. Dole Is Out of Control!

Text copyright © 2008 by Dan Gutman

Illustrations copyright © 2008 by Jim Paillot

Library of Congress Cataloging-in-Publication Data is available.
ISBN 978-0-06-134607-1 (pbk.) — ISBN 978-0-06-134608-8 (lib. bdg.)

Typography by Joel Tippie

❖

First Edition

12 13 LP/BR 20 19 18 17 16 15

Contents

The New PTA President

My name is A.J. and I hate school.

But you know what? Soon I won't have to go to school anymore for a long time. You know why? Because today is the first day of June!

Yay! June is the best month of the year because it's when summer starts! Yippee!

No school until September!

Me and the guys were putting our backpacks into our cubbies. It was Michael who started singing the best song in the history of the world.

"No more pencils!" sang Michael, who never ties his shoes.

"No more books!" sang Ryan, who will eat anything, even stuff that isn't food.

"No more teachers'!" sang Neil, who we call Neil the nude kid even though he wears clothes.

"Dirty looks!" I sang.

That's when Andrea came in. She is an annoying girl with curly brown hair who loves school. Andrea had on her mean face.

"Hey Andrea!" I said. "What's with the mean face? Are you mad because school is almost over?"

"No, Arlo," said Andrea, who calls me by my real name because she knows I don't like it. "That's not why I'm mad. Did you hear about the PTA election last night?"*

"No."

"My mother was running for president," Andrea said, "but she came in second. So she has to be vice president again."

"Big deal," I told Andrea. "If the president

---

*PTA stands for Parents who Talk A lot.

gets assassinated, then your mom will become president."

"Nobody assassinates PTA presidents, Arlo!" Andrea said, rolling her eyes.

"They do too!" I told her.

"Do not!"

"Do too!"

We went back and forth like that for a while. Sheesh, what a grouch! So what if her mom isn't PTA president? Andrea should take a chill pill.

I went to my seat, which is next to Ryan's.

"Where's Mrs. Daisy?" Ryan asked.

I looked around. Our teacher, Mrs. Daisy, was nowhere to be found. She usually gets to class early.

Mrs. Daisy used to be called Miss Daisy, but then she got married. Ladies become Mrs. when they get married. Nobody knows why.

Since Mrs. Daisy wasn't around, I crumpled up a piece of paper and threw it at Andrea. It bounced off her head.

"Arlo!" Andrea shouted. "Why did you do that?"

"Does there have to be a reason?"

Suddenly Mr. Klutz came running into the class. He's the principal of Ella Mentry School, and he has no hair at all. Most principals polish their shoes, but Mr. Klutz polishes his head.

"Mrs. Daisy will be late today," he said. "She has a doctor's appointment."

"Is Mrs. Daisy sick?" asked Emily, who is Andrea's crybaby friend. She looked all worried, like she does whenever anybody in the world is sick.

"She's fine," said Mr. Klutz. "Actually, I'm glad Mrs. Daisy is late, because the new PTA president wants to speak to you in private. I'd like to introduce—"

Mr. Klutz never had the chance to

finish his sentence. You'll never believe in a million hundred years who walked into the door.

Nobody! Because if you walked into a door, it would hurt. But you'll never believe who walked into the doorway.

It was Ryan's mom, Mrs. Dole!

Ryan's Mom Is Weird

Wow! Ryan's mom is the new PTA president!

"Congratulations, Mrs. Dole," said Mr. Klutz. "I'm sure you'll do a great job."

Mr. Klutz had to go to a meeting, so he left Ryan's mom to watch us.*

---

*This little star thing is called an asterisk. What a dumb word. They should just call it a star.

Mrs. Dole looked a lot like Ryan, except that she's a lady—and old. When she walked into our class, Ryan hid under his desk. I couldn't blame him. That's what I would do if my mom walked into the class. Parents should never come into your class, unless it's your birthday and they're bringing cupcakes for everybody. That's the first rule of being a kid.

"Wow, the president of the PTA is important," I whispered to Ryan. "That's almost like being president of the United States."

Ryan slid farther under his desk.

Andrea crossed her arms and said, "Humphf." Whenever somebody crosses their arms and says "Humphf," it means they're mad. Nobody knows why.

"Good morning!" said Mrs. Dole. "Are you kids excited about the end of school?"

"Yes!" said all the boys.

"No!" said all the girls.

"Are you excited about moving up to third grade?" Mrs. Dole asked.

"Yes!" said all the girls.

"No!" said all the boys.

"I was thinking. Wouldn't it be nice to give presents to Mrs. Daisy?" said Mrs. Dole. "She worked so hard for you all year. What would you like to give her?"

"I'll give her a skateboard," I said.

"That's what *you* want, Arlo!" Andrea said, rolling her eyes.

"Try to think of something Mrs. Daisy would want," Mrs. Dole said. "What does she like more than anything?"

"Flowers?" suggested Neil the nude kid.

"Shoes?" said Michael.

Suddenly I got the greatest idea in the history of the world.

"Bonbons!" I shouted.

"Yeah! Bonbons!" everybody agreed.

Bonbons are yummy chocolate treats. Mrs. Daisy eats them all the time. (Well, not while she's taking a shower. That would be weird.) She told us that she can eat a whole box of bonbons in one sitting.

Everybody thought giving Mrs. Daisy bonbons was a great idea. Neil the nude kid said I should get the No Bell Prize. That's a prize they give out to people who don't have bells.

"Okay. Your homework is to buy a

present for Mrs. Daisy and bring it to school tomorrow," Mrs. Dole said. "Any questions?"

"Are we going to get more homework in third grade?" asked Emily.

"I'm not sure," Mrs. Dole said. "Next year you'll learn the multiplication tables, and you're going to learn all about—"

Mrs. Dole didn't get the chance to finish her sentence, because that's when the strangest thing in the history of the world happened. She started crying!

"You kids are growing up so fast," Mrs. Dole blubbered. "I can hardly believe that my little baby Ryan is going to be a third grader. It seems like only yesterday he was in diapers."

Everybody looked at Ryan, who was still hiding under his desk.

"You wore diapers yesterday?" I asked him.

Mrs. Dole continued. "I remember when all my baby Ryan could say was 'Goo-goo-ga-ga,' and all he could do was pee. I had to wipe his little bottom for him. And now look at him."

Everybody looked at Ryan. Mrs. Dole grabbed a tissue from Mrs. Daisy's desk and blew her nose into it. Into the tissue, that is. Blowing your nose into a desk would be weird.

"I'm sorry. I get so emotional over my

baby," she said, and she ran out the door.

"Is she gone?" Ryan asked.

"Yeah, you can come out from under your desk now," Michael said.

"Your mom is weird," I told Ryan.

"I know," he replied. "She goes overboard a lot."

"She jumps out of boats?" I asked. "That's *really* weird."

There were no grown-ups in the room, so I got up and shook my butt at the class. Some of the kids laughed. Then me and Michael and Neil teased Ryan for all that peeing he did when he was a baby.

"That's what *all* babies do, Arlo," Andrea said.

"Well, I'm never having a baby," I told her.

"You can't have a baby, Arlo," Andrea said. "You're a boy!"

Whew! That was a relief. If babies just pee all day, I wouldn't want to have one anyway.

We had to stop talking about peeing because guess who came into the room at that very second?

It was Mrs. Daisy!

The Good Old Days

Mrs. Daisy came in with our reading teacher, Mr. Macky. They were holding hands and making goo-goo eyes at each other. Ugh! Disgusting! Mr. Macky said he would meet her in the teachers' lounge at lunchtime.*

---

*Footnotes usually have something to do with the thing in front of the asterisk. But not always.

Mrs. Daisy and Mr. Macky haven't been married very long. That's why they're so mushy with each other. Once they've been married for a few years, they'll stop doing all that mushy stuff. My parents have been married for like a century, and they hardly ever do mushy stuff.

"Are you sick, Mrs. Daisy?" asked Emily. "Mr. Klutz told us you went to the doctor."

"It was just a checkup," she replied. "Let's get to work. It's time for our Word of the Day. Today's word is 'unique.'"

"What does that mean?" asked Michael.

"I have no idea," said Mrs. Daisy, who doesn't know anything. "Does anybody know what 'unique' means?"

Andrea stuck her hand in the air, of course. Little Miss I-Know-Everything keeps a dictionary on her desk so she can look up words and show everybody how smart she is.

But Mrs. Daisy called on me instead.

"'Unique' means furniture that's really old," I said. "My mom has a unique table."

Everybody laughed even though I

didn't say anything funny.

"That's '*antique*,' dumbhead!" said Andrea. "'Unique' means something that's one of a kind."

"Oh, snap!" said Ryan.

"I knew that," I lied. "But a really old piece of furniture that's one of a kind is unique. It's a unique antique."

Nah-nah-nah boo-boo on Andrea! In her face! No wonder I'm in the gifted and talented program.

After we finished our Word of the Day, it was time for writing. I hate writing.

"The school year is almost over," Mrs. Daisy said, as she passed out pieces of paper. "Let's write about our favorite memories of second grade."

Mrs. Daisy told us to close our eyes and remember some of the nice things that happened since September.

"Remember the time Mrs. Roopy dressed up like Johnny Appleseed?" asked Andrea.

"Yeah," we all said. Mrs. Roopy is loopy.

"Remember the time we went on a field trip and Mr. Docker ate a bug?" asked Ryan.

"Yeah." Mr. Docker is off his rocker.

"Remember the time we drove that substitute teacher Ms. Todd crazy and she ran screaming into the parking lot?" Michael asked.

"Yeah." Ms. Todd is odd.

I couldn't decide if I should write about the time Mr. Klutz was hanging from the flagpole or the time Neil the nude kid's ferret pooped on Emily's head.

"Remember the time we had a food fight in the vomitorium?" Neil asked.

Yeah, that was great. I must admit, even though I hate school, we had some fun in second grade.

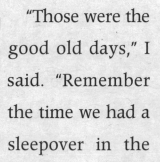

"Those were the good old days," I said. "Remember the time we had a sleepover in the natural history museum and a giant hissing cockroach crawled into Emily's sleeping bag?"

"That happened last week, Arlo!" Andrea said.

"So did your face," I told her.

Mrs. Daisy said she had to go to the ladies' room and that we should get started writing while she was gone. As soon as she left, I crumpled up a piece of paper and threw it at Andrea.

"You are so immature, Arlo!" Andrea said. "Maybe you'll get held back."

"Huh?" I asked. "What do you mean, 'held back'?"

"Didn't you know?" Andrea said. "They

take the bad kids and make them repeat the grade all over again. You're a bad kid, so you might be held back."

What?! Could they really do that? If I had known they make kids repeat a grade, I wouldn't have done so much bad stuff.

Everybody Loves Bonbons

The next morning, we had to go to the all-purpose room for an assembly. Mr. Klutz got up onstage with Officer Spence, our school security guard. Officer Spence was wearing a fireman costume.

"Today we're going to learn about fire safety," Mr. Klutz said. "Officer Spence is a trained firefighter."

"Fire is very dangerous, kids," said Officer Spence. "Does anybody know what you should do if your clothes catch on fire?"

I raised my hand, and Officer Spence pointed to me.

"If your clothes catch on fire," I said, "you should buy new clothes."

Everybody laughed even though I didn't say anything funny.

"Before you buy new clothes," said Officer Spence, "you should STOP, DROP, AND ROLL. Watch this."

Officer Spence did the most amazing thing in the history of the world. He

poured some stuff on his fireman costume. Then he took a lighter out of his
pocket and set himself on fire!

Officer Spence's fireman costume was
full of flames!

"STOP, DROP, AND ROLL!" shouted
Mr. Klutz. "STOP, DROP, AND ROLL!"

We all started chanting. Officer Spence

threw himself on the ground and covered his nose. Then he rolled all over the stage until the fire was out.

Officer Spence makes no sense.

He told us that we shouldn't go home and set ourselves on fire. We learned all kinds of other stuff about preventing fires too. Like you shouldn't ever set your brother or sister on fire.

When we got back to class, Ryan's mom was waiting for us. Ryan hid under his desk. Andrea's mom was waiting for us too. Andrea sat up even straighter than usual (if that's possible) and folded her hands so her mother would know how perfect she is.

The two PTA moms told Mrs. Daisy that the class had a surprise for her. We all went to our cubbies to get our presents. Then we lined up and put them on Mrs. Daisy's desk.

"I got you a box of bonbons," I told Mrs. Daisy.

"Hey, I got her a box of bonbons too!" said Michael.

"So did I!" said Emily.

"Me too!" said Neil the nude kid.

It turned out that just about everybody in class got Mrs. Daisy bonbons!

That's a lot of bonbons.

"Thank you so much," Mrs. Daisy said. "You know how much I love bonbons!"

"Everybody loves bonbons," said Emily.

"Why don't you open a box right now?" Michael suggested.

"Oh, I really shouldn't. I'm trying to eat healthier," Mrs. Daisy said. "Well, maybe just one."

Andrea's mom passed out bonbons to everyone. While we ate them, Mrs. Dole went to the front of the class.

"Part of my job as PTA president is to plan your graduation," she said. "You're going to wear caps and gowns, and there will be a guest speaker and a big cake, and you're going to get diplomas and—"

"Is all that really necessary?" asked Andrea's mom. "With all due respect, the children are just moving up to third grade."*

"Just moving up to third grade?" Mrs. Dole said. "This is an important milestone in the children's lives! Our babies are growing up so fast. Soon they'll be off to middle school. Before we know it, they'll be in high school. Then they'll be going off to college and I won't see my little boy anymore. . . ."

Mrs. Dole started sobbing. Ryan looked like he was gonna die. I thought his mom might tell more stories about Ryan peeing. But she just blew her nose in a

---

*"With all due respect" is grown-up talk for "I think you're stupid."

tissue and blubbered something about how much we grew since we were in kindergarten.

Andrea's mom rolled her eyes. I don't

think she likes Ryan's mom very much. But she can't do anything about it because Ryan's mom is the PTA president and she's only the vice president.

Finally, after a million hundred hours, the PTA moms left.

"Is my mother gone?" Ryan asked.

"Yeah," I told him. "You can come back up now."

Getting Ready for the Big Day

5

It was the last week of school, so we hardly learned anything. That was fine with me, because learning stuff is boring. But it was hard to concentrate. I kept thinking how in a few days we would be off for the summer.

Mrs. Daisy wasn't concentrating either.

She had a new hobby—knitting! She pretty much sat in the back of the room knitting while Ryan's mom helped us get ready for graduation. Sometimes Andrea's mom came in, too. But she spent most of the time rolling her eyes. Boy, she sure rolls her eyes a lot. Eye rolling must run in Andrea's family.

We had to do all kinds of stuff to get ready for graduation. Did you know that when you graduate, you have to wear a weird cap on your head that's shaped like a square? Nobody knows why. Mrs. Dole asked our art teacher, Ms. Hannah, to help us make the caps out of construction paper and cardboard. Ms. Hannah also helped us make graduation banners and signs to decorate the hallway.

On Thursday Mrs. Dole had us march from the gym to the playground behind the school so we would learn how to make a grand entrance for our parents. She made us practice over and over again until we got it right.

Did you ever hear of the graduation song? It's this song they always play at graduations. Mrs. Dole asked our music teacher, Mr. Loring, to play that song on an accordion while we marched around the playground. He told us the real name of the song is "Pomp and Circumstance," but nobody knows why.

The song doesn't have words. It goes like this:

Dum, dum-dum-dum, dum dum,
Dum, dum-dum-dum, dum.
Dum, dum-dum, dum-dum-dum,
Dum, dum-dum-dum-dum.

It's a dumb song, if you ask me. Songs are supposed to have words. So I made up words to the graduation song. They go like this:

I'm gra-ad-u-a-ting,

There's a square on my head.

Why is there a square on my head?

Be-cause I'm grad-u-a-ting.

You repeat that over and over again. While we were marching around the playground, I taught the words to everybody. Soon the whole class was singing. It was cool. Then Mrs. Dole told us to knock it off.

Practicing for graduation all morning was boring. I couldn't wait for lunch. Finally, after a million hundred hours, Mrs. Dole said it was time to go to the vomitorium to eat.

I sat at a table with the guys. Michael tried to juggle his Tater Tots. Neil the nude kid put cookies over his eyes. Ryan let us pour salt on his tongue. Andrea and her annoying friends sat at the next table talking about girly stuff, like what color dresses their dolls like to wear.

"What are you guys doing over the summer?" asked Ryan.

"I'm going to sleepaway camp," said Neil.

"I'm going to football camp," said Michael.

"I'm going to cooking camp," said Ryan.

"My family is going to rent a house at the beach," I said.

I didn't ask Andrea what she would be doing over the summer. She was probably going to learn her multiplication tables so she would be smarter than everybody in third grade.

Andrea was sitting there all quiet. I

figured she was still mad because her mom lost the PTA election.

"Are you still mad because your mom lost the PTA election?" I asked her.

"No," Andrea said. "I'm worried about Mrs. Daisy."

"What about her?" asked Emily, all concerned.

"Haven't you noticed?" Andrea said. "Mrs. Daisy has put on a lot of weight. She's getting fat."

"It must be all those bonbons we gave her," said Neil the nude kid.

"She's probably eating a box every night," Ryan said.

"That's not good for her," said Emily.

"It's all your fault, Arlo," Andrea said. "You were the one who thought of giving her bonbons."

Why is everything always my fault? I didn't force Mrs. Daisy to eat so many bonbons. What is Andrea's problem? I wish a truck full of bonbons would fall on her head.

6

The Greatest Day of My Life

Finally it was my favorite day of the year—the last day of school. Yay!

After we finished pledging the allegiance, Mrs. Daisy had us sing "Happy Birthday." But it wasn't anybody's birthday. We sang "Happy Birthday" to the kids in our class who have birthdays over

the summer. Like me. It is totally not fair that my birthday is in the summer. That means my mom can't bring in cupcakes for the class. Bummer in the summer!

We didn't learn anything all day. Mrs. Daisy had us clean the junk out of our desks. I found a peanut butter and jelly sandwich in the back that had been there for months. There was green stuff on it. I offered Ryan a quarter if he would take a bite of the sandwich, but he wouldn't.

Then we had to take our posters and artwork off the walls so we could bring them home. (The artwork, that is. We couldn't bring the walls home. That would be weird.)

Mrs. Dole came in and passed out yearbooks that had pictures of everybody in the whole school. We spent most of the morning signing each other's yearbooks. I wrote a little note in each one. Like "See you in third grade!" or "Summer rules!"

Andrea asked me if she could sign my yearbook. I didn't want her to, but Mrs. Dole was watching. So I let Andrea sign it.

She wrote, "I'll miss you, Arlo," above her picture.

"Oooooh!" Ryan said. "A.J. let Andrea sign his yearbook. They must be in *love*!"

"When are you gonna get married?" asked Michael.

If those guys weren't my best friends, I would hate them.

"Will you sign my yearbook, Arlo?" Andrea asked all sweetly, because she knew Mrs. Dole was watching.

This is what I wrote in Andrea's yearbook:

"I won't miss you . . . if I throw a rock at you!"

"That's mean!" Andrea said.

"So is your face," I told her.

Even though I hate school, I had to admit the last day was kind of sad. Mrs. Daisy told us that over the summer she and Mr. Macky were going to move to a bigger house in a different town. She wasn't even sure if she would come back to Ella Mentry School in September. Mrs. Daisy got all sniffly and had to blow her nose in a tissue. That made the girls get all sniffly too. Girls get sniffly real easy. Nobody knows why.

I kept looking at the clock, waiting for it to be three o' clock. But it was only one o'clock. Then it was one minute after one o'clock. Then it was two minutes after one o'clock. Then it was three minutes after one o'clock. The clock moves really slowly when you watch it. For a while, it looked like the hands were moving backwards.

Me and the guys threw crumpled-up paper at the girls, but Mrs. Daisy told us to knock it off.

After a million hundred hours, it was two o'clock. Isn't the word "o'clock" weird? What's up with that?

Me and the guys counted down the hours. The minutes. The seconds. Every second took a minute. Every minute took an hour. Every hour took a week. It was the longest day in the history of the world. I thought it would never end.

But finally the little hand was on the three and the big hand was on the twelve. You know what that means. Three o'clock!

The bell rang. We all went to hug Mrs. Daisy and then we bolted for the door.

We were free! Me and the guys ran out the front door like prisoners escaping from jail. Everybody was yelling and shouting and jumping.

No more pencils, no more books!
No more teachers' dirty looks!

It was the greatest day of my life.

Except for one thing.

But I'm not gonna tell you what it was.

Okay, okay, I'll tell you. But you have to read the next chapter first. So nah-nah-nah boo-boo on you.

Why Is There a Square on My Head?

7

There was only one bad thing about the last day of school. We had to come back after dinner for graduation! Bummer in the summer!*

---

*If you hide this book inside one of those Newbery Award–winning books, it will make you look a lot smarter.

My mom made me wear a tie. What's up with that? Why do boys have to wear this thing around their necks? Whoever thought up that idea should get the No Brain Award. That's an award they give out to people who don't have brains.

My dad helped me tie my tie while my mom combed my hair.

"You look so handsome!" my mom gushed, and she got all sniffly the way girls do.

"I expect you to be on your best behavior tonight, A.J.," my dad warned. "Nothing must go wrong."

I didn't even do anything wrong yet and already I was getting blamed! What could possibly go wrong, anyway? It was just a graduation.

We drove to school. Dad parked the car and we walked to the playground. Mrs. Dole and Andrea's mom were standing at the gate, greeting everyone.

As soon as we got inside the playground, I knew this was not going to be a normal graduation. There was a big stage set up with lights and a long banner that said CONGRATULATIONS, GRADUATES! Balloons were all over the place. And behind the stage was something really weird—a petting zoo, with goats and chickens and cows and bales of hay.

"Is all this really necessary?" my mom

asked Mrs. Dole. "With all due respect, what does a petting zoo have to do with graduating?"

"It represents the diversity of life on our fragile planet," Mrs. Dole replied. "As they grow up, children need to respect our animal friends."

I didn't know what she was talking about, but it was cool to see goats and chickens and cows in the playground. Andrea's mom rolled her eyes.

The teachers were sitting in the front row. I waved hello to Ms. Hannah, Mr. Docker, Mrs. Roopy, Miss Small, Ms. Coco, and all the others. Some of them were already sniffly and blowing their noses in tissues.

Mrs. Dole told the parents to sit down and the kids to go to the gym. When I got there, the guys had on ties, just like me. The girls had on party dresses. We had to put on the paper caps we made, and gowns too. I didn't want to wear a dumb gown. Gowns are for girls. But everybody else was putting one on, so I guess it was okay.

"Where did your mom get all those farm animals?" I asked Ryan.

"You can rent anything," Ryan said. "I guess she went to Rent-a-Farm-Animal."

After a million hundred hours, Mr.

Loring started playing the graduation song on the <u>accordion</u>. Mrs. Dole told us it was time to march out to the playground.

> *I'm gra-ad-u-a-ting,*
> *There's a square on my head. . . .*

It was windy outside. I had to hold on to my cap so it wouldn't blow away. As we marched into the playground, our parents started clapping and taking pictures like we were movie stars. I sat between Michael and Ryan.

"I hope my mom doesn't go overboard," Ryan whispered.

I didn't think that would happen, because there weren't any boats around. Mrs. Dole walked onto the stage. There was a big bowl in front of her. It was about the size of a garbage can cover, and it was on a little stand.

"Welcome parents, teachers, and students!" Mrs. Dole announced. "Let's begin the ceremony by lighting the eternal flame."

She took a lighter out of her pocket and lit something in the bowl in front of her. Flames shot up in the air.

"This flame represents the eternal quest for knowledge that will forever burn within you," Mrs. Dole told us.

I didn't know what she was talking about, but fire is cool. Maybe we would get to toast marshmallows later.

After she lit the eternal flame, Mrs. Dole gave a speech. I don't remember much of it, but I think she told us to look both ways before putting on sunscreen and to always wear a bike helmet if we went running with scissors.

"Third grade can be scary," Mrs. Dole said. "But remember how frightened you were on your first day of kindergarten? My little baby Ryan was so scared to go to school that he peed in his pants. I remember it like it was yesterday."

"You peed in your pants yesterday?" I asked Ryan.

He was hiding under his chair. Man, that's what I would do if my mom just told hundreds of strangers that I peed in my pants yesterday.

After Mrs. Dole's speech, I thought we would get our diplomas. But no! A marching band came out of the gym and played that song about going to the YMCA. Then a big cake was wheeled out in front of the stage. All right! I love cake!

But we didn't get to eat it yet. We had to sit and listen to more talking. Mrs. Dole grabbed the microphone again.

"Being PTA president is a big responsibility," she said. "Being president of anything is a big responsibility. That's why I'm very excited to introduce our special guest speaker. He's also a president. Please welcome the former president of the United States . . . Mr. Bill Clinton!"

8

Blah Blah Blah Blah Blah

Wow! A president of the United States was going to talk to us! Double wow!

Everybody clapped. A guy with white hair came out of the gym and went over to the microphone.

I whispered to Ryan, "How did your mom get President Clinton to come to our graduation?"

"I guess she went to Rent-a-President," he said.

Everybody finished clapping, and President Clinton started to speak. I didn't catch every word he said, but it went something like this:

"Blah blah blah blah blah blah blah blah blah blah blah blah blah blah blah

blah blah blah blah blah blah blah blah
blah blah blah blah blah blah blah blah
blah blah blah blah blah blah blah blah
blah blah this is so boring blah blah blah
blah blah blah blah blah blah blah blah
blah blah blah blah blah blah blah blah
blah blah blah blah blah blah blah blah
blah blah blah blah blah blah blah blah
blah blah blah blah blah blah blah is he
almost done blah blah blah blah blah
blah blah blah blah blah blah blah blah
blah blah blah blah blah blah blah blah
blah blah blah blah blah blah blah blah
blah blah blah blah blah blah blah blah
blah blah blah blah blah blah blah he
can't go on much longer blah blah blah

blah blah blah blah blah blah blah blah blah blah blah blah blah blah blah blah blah blah blah I think he's almost finished blah blah blah blah blah blah blah blah blah blah blah blah blah blah blah blah blah blah blah blah blah blah blah blah blah blah blah blah blah blah blah blah I think I'm gonna die blah blah blah blah blah blah blah blah blah blah blah . . ."

Man, that guy sure can talk! President Clinton went on for about a million hundred hours. Everybody clapped really loud at the end because we were so glad he was finished.[*]

---

[*]Try this science experiment. Put a banana on your head. See how long it takes for somebody to notice that you have a banana on your head. Record the results.

I figured we were going to get our diplomas and eat cake next, but we didn't. Mrs. Dole got back up onstage and stood next to President Clinton.

"And now, ladies and gentlemen," she said, "I would like to introduce another surprise guest. Please direct your attention over your heads. . . ."

We all looked up. I didn't see anything at first. But then I saw it. There was a helicopter hovering up there! It was coming down right over us!

I held on to my cap so it wouldn't blow away. The helicopter landed at the other end of the playground. It was cool!

Nothing happened for a few minutes.

Then this weird
purple smoke started
pouring out from under
the stage. The sounds of
drums pounded out of the speakers.
Laser beams shot all over the place.

Suddenly two guys jumped out of the
helicopter, ran up onstage, and started
dancing around. They were wearing football jerseys and baseball caps.

Then another guy hopped out of the helicopter and ran up onstage. He had on a baseball cap too, and he was wearing this big purple cape with sequins all over it.

It was Mr. Hynde, our old music teacher!

Mrs. Dole Goes Overboard

9

Mr. Hynde is the coolest guy in the history of the world! He used to be a plain old music teacher; but then he went on that TV show *American Idol,* and now he's a famous rapper.

Mr. Hynde's homeboys started yelling into the microphones.

"And now, appearing live and in person at Ella Mentry School is the one . . . the only . . . Jam Master Hynde, the One-Man Funky Groove Machine! Give it up, y'all! Mr. Hynde is in the house!"

The drums got louder. The lights got brighter.

"Yo! What up, homeys?" Mr. Hynde shouted. "Put your hands together! I'm here to rock your world! So get on your feet! The only way to get down is to get up!"

We all stood up and started clapping. Mr. Hynde danced around. Then he threw off his purple cape and started rapping:

Now, my name's Hynde, and I'm here to remind.

Summer's here, and it's time to unwind.

Word on the street is you're graduatin',

so I dropped in for some congratulatin'.

You're gettin' so big, movin' up to third grade.

Bet you think you got it all made.

But lemme just give you a little advice:

You better not be naughty, you better be nice,

You better brush your teeth, and here's the

>   *real deal,*

you better wash your hands before you eat a meal.

You better clean your room, and you better be kind.

Don't stare at the sun unless you wanna go blind.

Better mind your manners and stay outta danger.

Don't tease your brother or take candy from

>   *a stranger.*

Early to bed and early to rise,

don't touch the paint until it dries.

Sticks and stones may break your bones

but not like killer robot clones.

Now, here's what I'm really tryin' to rap

while you sit there in your gown and cap.

Some days you'll feel sad, some days you'll

> *feel happy,*

some nights you'll feel mad, some nights

> *you'll feel crappy.*

But I ain't jivin', and I ain't jestin'.

That's just what makes life interestin'.

Anyway, that's what I got to say

on this, your graduation day.

You kids are cool, you're in the groove,

so now it's time to bust a move!

Everybody was going crazy. One of the guys in the marching band gave

President Clinton a saxophone, and he started playing it. Mr. Hynde danced around and drummed on Mr. Klutz's head like it was a <u>bongo</u>.

Mr. Hynde is out of his mind!

Finally Mr. Hynde and President Clinton climbed into the helicopter and flew away.

That had to be the end of it. We were sure to get our diplomas and cake now.

But no!

Mrs. Dole raised her arm, and a million hundred white doves went flying up in the air! It was amazing! I was glad I had a square on my head just in case one of those doves pooped.

Mrs. Dole is out of control!

"Where did all those doves come from?" I asked Ryan.

"Rent-a-Dove," he said.

After the doves were gone, Mrs. Dole raised her arm again, and a rocket went flying up in the air over the school. It exploded in a million hundred directions, and the next thing we knew, the sky was filled with fireworks! It was cool!

"Where did your mom get the—"

"Rent-a-Fireworks," said Ryan.

At the end of the fireworks show, we heard this huge roar up in the sky. I thought it was a hurricane or something. But then six jet planes zoomed right over our school, in formation! It was awesome! I had to hold on to my cap so it wouldn't fly off my head.

"Where did your mom—"

"Rent-a-Blue-Angels-Flyover," said Ryan. "See, I told you my mom goes overboard."

I didn't know what he was talking

about. His mom didn't fall out of a boat or anything. But it didn't matter, because after the jet planes flew away, Mr. Klutz got up onstage to make a speech.

"Second graders," he said, "life is about challenges. Early in the school year I challenged you to read a million pages, and you did it. So I had to dress up in a gorilla suit. Next I challenged you to do a million math problems, and you did it. So I had to kiss a pig. Then I challenged you to write a million spelling words, and you did it. So I had to pogo-stick down Main Street in a turkey costume. Finally I chal-lenged you to get the highest reading score in the county, and you did it. So I had to paint my head orange. You always met my challenges. Now I have one last challenge for you."

"What is it?" somebody yelled.

"If you kids line up in an orderly fashion and come onstage for your diplomas," said Mr. Klutz, "I will let you throw your caps up in the air."

All right! Throwing stuff is fun! That's the first rule of being a kid. At school, grown-ups are constantly telling us we're not allowed to throw stuff.

It was time for the big moment. Finally we were going to get our diplomas, throw our caps in the air, and eat cake. We all lined up next to the stage. Mr. Klutz read our names one by one. Mrs. Dole handed each of us a diploma. The parents were tripping all over each other trying to take pictures.

"Congratulations!" Mrs. Dole hollered after she handed out the last diploma. "You are now officially third graders!"

Yippee! I'd been waiting all year for this moment. Finally I was allowed to throw something at school. I took the cap off my head and winged it as high and as far as I could.

And you'll never believe in a million hundred years what happened next.

Throwing Up

I threw my cap up like a Frisbee, really high and far. And then, like a Frisbee, it caught the wind and curved back toward me. I thought it might hit the stage—but instead it hit the bowl that held the eternal flame!

The bowl fell off its stand and onto the ground. My cap caught on fire, and everybody started freaking out.

"Quick! Somebody get a fire extinguisher!" Mr. Klutz yelled.

Mrs. Dole went running off to look for a fire extinguisher. Meanwhile, the wind whipped the flame and sparks around. The next thing we knew, the CONGRATULA-TIONS, GRADUATES! banner was on fire.

"Forget the fire extinguisher!" Mr. Klutz yelled. "Call the fire department!"

The banner was whipping around in the wind, and soon it didn't say CONGRAT-ULATIONS, GRADUATES! anymore. All it said was RAT DATES, because the rest of it had burned up.

Everybody was freaking out because there were sparks flying all over the place. Some of the sparks were falling on the hay at the petting zoo.

"Excuse me," I said to Emily.

"What do you want, A.J.?" Emily asked, like she was all annoyed.

"I just wanted to let you know that you're on fire," I told her.

It was true! Somehow a spark must have landed on Emily's gown, and her gown was going up in flames.

Emily freaked out and went running around like she was, well, on fire.

Which she was.

"HELP! I'M ON FIRE!" Emily screamed.

"STOP, DROP, AND ROLL!" everybody shouted.

Emily stopped, dropped, and rolled. But the only problem was that she rolled right into the table that was holding the giant cake!

The table toppled over and the cake slid off—landing right on top of Emily! The good news was that the cake put out the fire. The bad news was that our cake was ruined.

"Five-second rule!" I shouted, and a bunch of us ran over to grab chunks of cake off the playground before five seconds were up. Mmmm! It was great!

Meanwhile, the hay in the petting zoo had ignited, and the cows and chickens and goats were mooing and squawking and freaking out. One of the cows knocked down the wooden fence, and soon all the animals were running around the playground.

You should have been there! It was a real Kodak moment. But nobody was taking pictures because all the parents were busy trying to avoid being trampled by the cows and goats.

"Remain calm!" screamed Mrs. Dole as she ran around, spraying a fire extinguisher.

"Run for your lives!" shouted Neil the nude kid as a goat chased him across the playground.

I was wondering if third grade would be canceled if the school burned down. But it didn't matter, because soon there was a siren coming down the street. A fire truck pulled up, and Officer Spence hopped off. He attached a hose to a hydrant in the street and sprayed water all over the place. Everybody got soaked.

I thought it was all over; but in the middle of the playground, I saw Andrea's mom and Ryan's mom yelling at each other.

"This is all your fault!" Andrea's mom shouted. "You and your stupid graduation!"

"How was I supposed to know somebody would knock over the eternal flame?" shouted Ryan's mom.

The next thing we knew, the two PTA moms were wrestling each other on the ground and pulling each other's hair! And we got to see it live and in person!

"See," I said to Andrea, "I told you PTA presidents get assassinated. Your mom is trying to kill Ryan's mom so she can become president."

Mr. Klutz broke up the fight. He told us to line up near Mrs. Daisy. Some of the parents went to round up the animals.

Mrs. Daisy didn't look very good. Her hair was all messy.

"I don't feel very well," she said. "I think I need to sit—"

But Mrs. Daisy never had the chance to finish her sentence, because at that moment the most amazing thing in the history of the world happened.

Mrs. Daisy fainted!

Passing Out and Making Out

11

Me and the guys caught Mrs. Daisy just before she was about to hit the ground. Her eyes were closed and she was all limp, like a rag doll.

"Wake up!" Ryan shouted. "Wake up, Mrs. Daisy!"

"She can't hear you," said Neil.

"Is she dead?" I asked.

"She just fainted, Arlo," Andrea said.

"Whenever a girl faints in the movies," I said, "somebody slaps her in the face and she wakes up."

"You should slap her, A.J.," said Michael.

"I'm not slapping Mrs. Daisy," I said. "I'll get kicked out of school. Why don't you slap her?"

"I'm not slapping her," Michael said. "You're the one who thought of giving her all those bonbons. That's probably why she fainted. *You* should slap her."

"You slap her!" I shouted.

"No, you slap her!"

"Tell you what," I finally said. "Let's both slap her."

Me and Michael were about to slap Mrs. Daisy when Mr. Macky came running over to us. We decided to let him slap her. But he didn't. He was holding a wet handkerchief, and he held it against Mrs. Daisy's forehead.

"Give her air!" he shouted, which didn't make any sense because none of us had any air to give her. Who carries around air? Where would we get air anyway? Rent-a-Air?

"This is all your fault, Arlo!" said Andrea. "You knocked over the eternal flame! They'll probably make you repeat second grade for this."

"Mr. Klutz told us to throw our caps up in the air!" I yelled. "I didn't mean to knock over the eternal flame! Why do I get blamed for everything?"

Officer Spence came rushing over to us.

"What happened?" he asked.

"She fainted," said Mr. Macky.

"It's because she ate so many bon-bons," Andrea told Officer Spence. "She got fatter and fatter. I bet all that sugar made her pass out."

Then Officer Spence did the most amazing thing in the history of the world. He leaned over and kissed Mrs. Daisy! On the lips! Right in front of her husband!

"Ewww!" I said. "They're making out! Mr. Macky, are you going to let Officer Spence kiss your wife? You should punch him in the nose. That's what guys do in the movies when they catch somebody kissing their wife."

"He's giving her mouth-to-mouth resuscitation, dumbhead!" said Andrea.

I didn't know what mouth-to-mouth resuscitation was, but it looked a lot like kissing to me.

I was trying to think of something mean to say to Andrea when Mrs. Daisy opened her eyes.

"Where am I?" she asked.

"You're in the playground," said Officer Spence. "You're going to be fine. Did you eat a lot of bonbons recently?"

"No," Mrs. Daisy said, "I gave almost all of them away."

"Then how did you get so fat?" I asked.

"Because . . ."

"Because we're going to have a baby!" said Mr. Macky.

WHAT????!!!!

12

The Perfect Baby Name

Mr. Macky told us that Mrs. Daisy is going to have a baby in the fall. She was waiting for the right moment to tell us the big news.

"So that's why you had a doctor's appointment!" said Andrea.

"And that's why you're moving to a

bigger house!" said Michael.

"And that's why you've been knitting and trying to eat healthier!" said Emily.

"And that's why you fainted!" I said.

"That's right," said Mrs. Daisy.

The girls were all excited and giggly because girls always get excited and giggly whenever they find out somebody is going to have a baby. Nobody knows why. They crowded around to hug Mrs. Daisy, touch her stomach, and argue over whether the baby would be a boy or a girl.

Next the girls started thinking up baby names, because that's what you're supposed to do when you find out somebody is going to have a baby. The girls decided the baby should be named Michelle.

"What about you guys?" asked Mr. Macky. "What do you think we should name the baby?"

Hmmm. I looked around. Firefighters were still hosing off the petting zoo. That's when I came up with the best baby name in the history of the world.

"Hydrant," I suggested.

"HYDRANT?" everyone shouted.

I said that Hydrant would be a great name for a baby, because it would be antique. There was probably no other kid in the world named Hydrant. Besides, Hydrant would be the perfect name

because the only thing babies can do is pee. Sort of like a hydrant.

All in all, I thought graduation went pretty well, except that I knocked over the eternal flame, Emily caught on fire, the petting zoo animals escaped, and the school almost burned down. But stuff like that happens all the time at Ella Mentry School.

Maybe I shouldn't have thrown my cap up in the air. Maybe we'll get another cake. Maybe the parents will be able to round up the cows and goats and chickens. Maybe Ryan's mom will stop jumping out of boats. Maybe Andrea's mom will become PTA president. Maybe Officer Spence will stop kissing married women. Maybe Ryan will stop hiding under his desk whenever his mom is around. Maybe Mrs. Daisy and Mr. Macky will name their baby Hydrant. Maybe by

September everybody will forget what happened at graduation. Maybe we'll be able to talk Mr. Klutz into letting us have another graduation at the end of third grade.

But it won't be easy!

Check out the **My Weird School** series!

#1: Miss Daisy Is Crazy!

The first book in the hilarious series stars A.J., a second grader who hates school—and can't believe his teacher hates it too!

#2: Mr. Klutz Is Nuts!

A.J. can't believe his crazy principal wants to climb to the top of the flagpole!

#3: Mrs. Roopy Is Loopy!

The new librarian thinks she's George Washington one day and Little Bo Peep the next!

#4: Ms. Hannah Is Bananas!

The art teacher wears clothes made from pot holders. Worse than that, she's trying to make A.J. be partners with yucky Andrea!

#5: Miss Small Is off the Wall!

The gym teacher is teaching A.J.'s class to juggle scarves, balance feathers, and do everything *but* play sports!

#6: Mr. Hynde Is Out of His Mind!

The music teacher plays bongo drums on the principal's bald head! But does he have what it takes to be a real rock-and-roll star?

#7: Mrs. Cooney Is Loony!

The school nurse is everybody's favorite—but is she hiding a secret identity?

#8: Ms. LaGrange Is Strange!

The new lunch lady talks funny—and why is she writing secret messages in the mashed potatoes?

#9: Miss Lazar Is Bizarre!

What kind of grown-up *likes* cleaning throw-up? Miss Lazar is the weirdest custodian in the world!

#10: Mr. Docker Is off His Rocker!

The science teacher alarms and amuses A.J.'s class with his wacky experiments and nutty inventions.

#11: Mrs. Kormel Is Not Normal!
A.J.'s school bus gets a flat tire, then becomes hopelessly lost at the hands of the wacky bus driver.

#12: Ms. Todd Is Odd!
Ms. Todd is subbing, and A.J. and his friends are sure she kidnapped Miss Daisy so she could take over her job.

#13: Mrs. Patty Is Batty!
A little bit of spookiness and a lot of humor add up to the best trick-or-treating adventure ever!

#14: Miss Holly Is Too Jolly!
Mistletoe means kissletoe, the worst tradition in the history of the world!

#15: Mr. Macky Is Wacky!
Mr. Macky expects A.J. and his friends to read stuff about the presidents...and even dress up like them! He's taking Presidents' Day way too far!

#16: Ms. Coco Is Loco!
It's Poetry Month and the whole school is poetry crazy, thanks to Ms. Coco. She talks in rhyme! She thinks boys should have feelings! Is she crazy?

#17: Miss Suki Is Kooky!
Miss Suki is a very famous author who writes about endangered animals. But when her pet raptor gets loose during a school visit, it's the kids who are endangered!

#18: Mrs. Yonkers Is Bonkers!
Mrs. Yonkers builds a robot substitute teacher to take her place for a day!

#19: Dr. Carbles Is Losing His Marbles!
Dr. Carbles, the president of the board of education, is fed up with Mr. Klutz and wants to fire him. Will A.J. and his friends be able to save their principal's job?

#20: Mr. Louie Is Screwy!
When the hippie crossing guard, Mr. Louie, puts a love potion in the water fountain, everyone at Ella Mentry School falls in love!

#21: Ms. Krup Cracks Me Up!
A.J. thinks that nothing can possibly be as boring as a sleepover in the natural history museum. But anything can happen when Ms. Krup is in charge.